THE ADVENTURES OF Captain Pugwash

D1079464

The Stowaway Sheep

RED FOX

A Red Fox Book

Published by Random House Children's Books
20 Vauxhall Bridge Road, London SW1V 2SA

A division of The Random House Group Ltd
London Melbourne Sydney Auckland
Johannesburg and agencies throughout the world

The Adventures of Captain Pugwash
Created by John Ryan
© Britt Allcroft (Development) Limited 2000
All rights worldwide Britt Allcroft (Development) Limited
CAPTAIN PUGWASH is a trademark of Britt Allcroft (Development) Limited
THE BRITT ALLCROFT COMPANY is a trademark of The Britt Allcroft Company plc

Cover illustration by Ian Hillyard
Inside illustrations by Red Central Limited

Text adapted by Sally Byford from the original TV story

1 3 5 7 9 10 8 6 4 2

This book is sold subject to the condition that it shall not, by way of trade or
otherwise, be lent, resold, hired out, or otherwise circulated without the publisher's
prior consent in any form of binding or cover other than that in which it is published
and without a similar condition including this condition being imposed on the
subsequent purchaser.

THE RANDOM HOUSE GROUP Limited Reg. No. 954009

www.randomhouse.co.uk

ISBN 0 09 940815 5

Captain Pugwash was feeling very pleased with himself. Last night, he'd led a daring attack on the Flying Dustman, the ship belonging to Cut-throat Jake, his oldest and meanest enemy. While Cut-throat Jake's men were sleeping, Captain Pugwash and his crew had crept aboard and stolen a treasure chest full of gold coins.

Pugwash was so pleased he gave each of his crew a gold coin.

Willy had spent his gold
coin at Portobello Market
on what he thought was a
very funny-looking dog.
He proudly put his new pet
on a lead and returned to the harbour.
   "No animals are allowed on ship by order
         of the Captain," said the Mate.
           "So get rid of that sheep!"

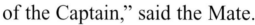

                 "It's not a sheep. It's a dog," said
                 Willy. "His name is Rover."
                 The Mate shook his
                 head and left.
                   "Don't worry," Jonah
                   whispered to Willy.
                   "I'll help you
                   sneak him
                   aboard."

From high up in the crow's nest, Tom, the cabin boy, had spotted a sail in the distance.

"Captain!" he called. "It's the Flying Dustman!"

"Nonsense," said Pugwash. Then he looked through his telescope and saw the enemy ship. "Blundering bloaters! Er... hoist the anchor! Raise the sails! All hands on deck!" he cried.

Soon the Black Pig had left the harbour and was sailing out to sea.

"We've given Jake the slip again," said Pugwash proudly.

Tom was not so sure. "He could be hiding on the other side of Cutlass Island, and planning an attack," he said.

"T-t-tottering turtles," said Pugwash. "I've just had a thought – he could be hiding on the other side of the island. Keep a look out, Tom."

Tom smiled. "Aye, aye, Captain," he said.

On board the Flying Dustman, Cut-throat Jake was making plans to surprise the crew of the Black Pig.

"We'll wait until it's dark and he's far away from help," chuckled Jake, "and then we'll attack!"

Dook, Swine and Stinka cheered loudly.

"And then," growled Jake, "we'll show Pugwash the horrible things that happen to people who steal my treasure. Ha, ha, ha!"

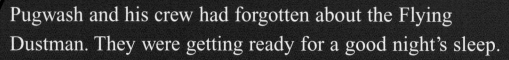

Pugwash and his crew had forgotten about the Flying
Dustman. They were getting ready for a good night's sleep.

The Mate climbed into his hammock. "Oh no!" he cried. "It's
that sheep!" He had found Rover, who was hidden under the
covers, chewing at his night-cap.

"He's a dog," squeaked Willy, but no one took any notice.

"The Captain will be cross if he finds an animal on the
ship," said the Mate. "We must hide him quick."

But Rover had other ideas. When the crew tried to grab him,
he bared his teeth and lowered his head, ready to attack.

Willy, Jonah and the Mate took one look at Rover's sharp
horns. "Run!" they cried, and bolted into a cupboard. There,
they huddled together in the dark, while Rover butted the door.

Pugwash came up on deck to search for Tom. "Where's my bedtime cocoa?" he called.

But Tom was nowhere to be seen. Instead, Pugwash found himself face to face with a very angry sheep.

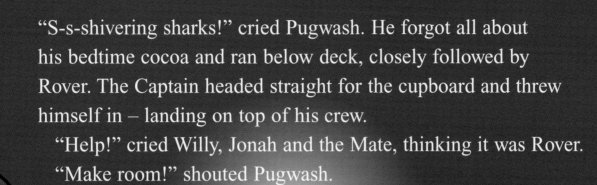

"S-s-shivering sharks!" cried Pugwash. He forgot all about his bedtime cocoa and ran below deck, closely followed by Rover. The Captain headed straight for the cupboard and threw himself in – landing on top of his crew.

"Help!" cried Willy, Jonah and the Mate, thinking it was Rover.

"Make room!" shouted Pugwash.

While this was happening,
the Flying Dustman had
caught up with the Black Pig.

Jake and his crew swung
aboard.

"Ah ha! The Black Pig's
mine now!" bellowed Jake.
"And first of all I'm going
to find my treasure and
steal it back."

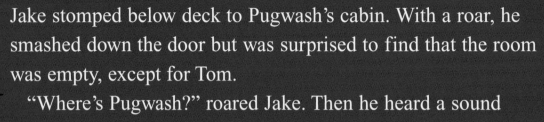

Jake stomped below deck to Pugwash's cabin. With a roar, he smashed down the door but was surprised to find that the room was empty, except for Tom.

"Where's Pugwash?" roared Jake. Then he heard a sound coming from the Captain's bed.

"I wouldn't look in there if I were you," said Tom.

But Jake had already ripped the curtains apart. He was sure he would find Captain Pugwash, cowering in a corner. He got a great shock when he saw a sheep there instead, chewing on some carrot tops.

Jake roared more loudly than ever, and Rover went wild. He launched himself at Cut-throat Jake.

Jake panicked and
dashed up onto the deck to join
his crew. Rover charged after him.
   Dook, Swine and Stinka were
so confused that they followed
Cut-throat Jake as he fled from the sheep.
"Help!" they all cried, as they ran round and
round the deck. But there was nowhere they could
escape – except overboard!

"Aaargh!" With a cry, Dook, Swine, Stinka and Cut-throat Jake leapt into the sea. Splash! The ugly crew struggled in the water, yelling and cursing with rage.

Tom opened the cupboard door and Captain Pugwash, Jonah, Willy and the Mate landed in a heap at his feet.

"S-s-stuttering starfish," said Pugwash. "Where have you been?"

"Cut-throat Jake and his crew came aboard," Tom explained. "But it's all right now, thanks to Rover." Then he told them the whole story.

While Cut-throat Jake and his crew were splashing around in the sea, Pugwash and his crew helped themselves to the rest of the treasure on the Flying Dustman.

Afterwards, Captain Pugwash held a party to celebrate. "Congratulations, everyone," he said. "I had it all planned from the start, of course…"

Pugwash's speech came to a sudden
end when he heard a loud bleat from
the doorway.

"HELP!" shouted Pugwash and his crew, and they leapt up onto the table and clung together, trembling with fear.

Tom was the only one who wasn't scared, but then he had discovered how to keep Rover as gentle as a lamb – by feeding him plenty of carrot tops!